The Emerald Princess Follows a Unicorn

THE JEWEL KINGDOM

The Emerald Princess Follows a Unicorn

JAHNNA N. MALCOLM

Illustrations by Paul Casale

SCHOLASTIC INC.
NEW YORK   TORONTO   LONDON   AUCKLAND   SYDNEY
MEXICO CITY   NEW DELHI   HONG KONG

For Susan, Jack, and Sir Chase
With love and thanks

ISBN 0-590-97879-9

12 11 10 9 8 7 6 5 4 3 2   9/9 0 1 2 3 4/0

Printed in the U.S.A.   40
First Scholastic printing, March 1999

CONTENTS

The Emerald Princess Follows a Unicorn

THE JEWEL KINGDOM

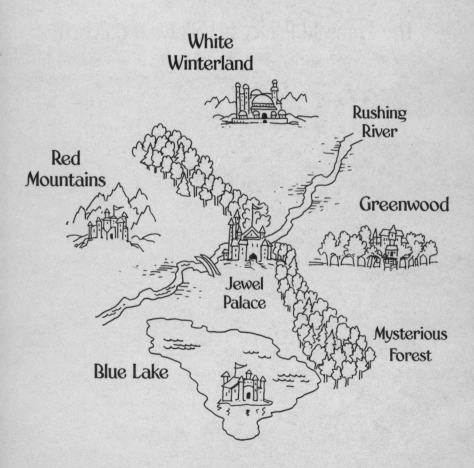

White
Winterland

Rushing
River

Red
Mountains

Greenwood

Jewel
Palace

Mysterious
Forest

Blue Lake

The Story Quilt

—◆—

 "Look at this!" cried Princess Emily. The Emerald Princess held up a piece of golden cloth. "Won't this make the perfect border for our quilt?"

The four Jewel Princesses were gathered at Emily's palace in the Greenwood. Their parents, King Regal and Queen Jemma, were celebrating their wedding anniversary the next day. The

1

princesses had decided to make them a quilt as a gift. It was to be a map of the Jewel Kingdom. Each princess was sewing a patch that showed something special about her land.

"It's beautiful," her sister Princess Sabrina said. Sabrina was the Sapphire Princess and ruled Blue Lake. "Mother and Father will love it."

"It makes the quilt look just like one of those old maps in Father's study," remarked the Ruby Princess, Roxanne. She lived in the Red Mountains.

"Don't you think you should start working on your patch, Emily?" Demetra asked quietly. "After all, the anniversary celebration is tomorrow." Demetra was the oldest of the princesses and always dressed in white. Her kingdom was called the White Winterland.

Emily pointed to a beautiful white Unicorn at the window, looking down on the forest floor far below. "I think my patch should show off one of Arden's magical powers, but I can't decide which one."

Arden the Unicorn was Emily's best friend in the Greenwood. Emily rarely went anywhere without her.

"I always knew a Unicorn's horn was special," Princess Sabrina said, "but I didn't realize it held magic powers, too."

"Oh, yes," Emily said. "Unicorns can be very magical. Right, Arden?"

"That's true." Arden trotted over and stood beside the Emerald Princess. "Our magic just grows stronger as we grow older."

Emily beamed proudly. "Arden can even fly!"

"Fly?" Princess Roxanne repeated. "You mean, like Hapgood?"

Hapgood the Dragon was Roxanne's best friend and advisor. He lived with her at her palace in the Red Mountains.

"Arden has flown to the highest tower of the Emerald Palace three times," Emily boasted. "Isn't that right, Arden?"

Arden looked at the floor. "We Unicorns aren't really supposed to fly until we're all grown-up."

"But I told Arden there's no harm in trying before then," Emily added. "And she did it."

"What else can you do?" Princess Demetra asked the Unicorn.

"Well, there's the power of light," Arden said shyly. "I have been able to use that."

Emily draped one arm proudly across the Unicorn's neck. "Whenever we're in the woods at night, I never take a lantern. I just use Arden's magic horn to light our way."

"That seems like a waste of magic," Demetra murmured.

Emily shrugged. "If magic is there, why not use it?"

Sabrina tucked a strand of her blond hair behind one ear. "I guess I think of magic as something very rare and precious. Something to use only when it's needed."

"Don't be so serious," Emily laughed. "We're just playing around."

"If you play with fire, you can get burned," Roxanne warned.

"Oh, Roxanne, you're not scared of magic, are you?" Emily teased as she crossed the room to pick up a basket of gold thread.

Roxanne shook her jet-black hair. "I'm

not afraid of magic. I respect its power."

Emily sighed loudly. "You are being silly. Magic is not as unusual as you think." Just then Princess Emily tripped over the edge of a rug. The basket of thread went flying and she fell to the floor.

"Ow!" Emily cried, clutching her foot. "I think I twisted my ankle."

"Don't move," Sabrina urged, kneeling beside her sister.

Roxanne bolted for the door. "I'll call for Nana Woodbine to come help."

"No, don't!" Emily cried as she tried to stand. "Arden, will you help me? Use your magic horn."

"I'll try." Arden moved close to the princess.

Emily nudged Sabrina. "Unicorns can heal people with the touch of their horn. You'll see."

Arden carefully lowered her head so that her golden horn was just touching Emily's ankle.

Emily held her breath and waited for her ankle to feel better. But nothing happened.

"Come on, Arden," Emily urged. "My sisters are going to think you don't have any magic at all."

"I'm trying," Arden said. She squeezed her eyes closed and touched Emily's ankle with her horn again.

Still nothing.

Finally Sabrina said, "Look, Arden, I have a strip of extra material. I'll dip it in some water and wrap Emily's ankle. You don't have to worry."

Arden bowed her head. "Thank you, Princess," she said softly. Then the Unicorn turned and hurried out of the room. She didn't even pause to look back at Emily.

Emily watched her friend leave and murmured, "What's wrong with Arden?"

"I think she's embarrassed," Sabrina whispered.

Emily's green eyes widened. "But why?"

"I'm not sure," Sabrina said softly. "But I think your Unicorn may have lost her magic powers."

The Magic Disappears

 After Sabrina wrapped her ankle, Princess Emily limped out of the room in search of Arden. Could a Unicorn really lose her magic powers? It didn't seem possible.

Emily left her palace and searched the forest nearby. She found the Unicorn hiding in a narrow thicket.

"What's wrong, Arden?" the princess

asked her friend. "Why are you so upset?"

Arden turned her beautiful white head to look at Emily. Tears filled her brown eyes. "I've lost my magic powers."

"But why? How did it happen?" Emily asked.

Arden shook her head. "I don't know why. All I know is that my powers are gone."

"All of them?" Emily asked.

Arden nodded miserably. "It's just like you said. I don't have any magic at all."

"Oh, Arden," Emily gasped, putting her hands to her mouth. "I was only joking when I said that." She hurried to her friend's side and wrapped her arms around Arden's neck. "I would never do anything to hurt you. You're my best friend."

Arden stared at the ground. "Your best friend has let you down."

"No, you haven't." Emily walked in a small circle in front of Arden. "See? My ankle feels better already!"

"But it wasn't my magic that cured your ankle," Arden said softly. "My magic has gone away."

Emily put her hands on her hips. "There's got to be a way to fix this, like a spell or something."

Arden raised her head. "The only spells I know come from *The Great Book of Magic*."

"That big leather book in the palace library?" Emily asked. "It's so heavy, I can barely lift it."

"That's because it holds so much information," Arden explained. "Most of the spells ever invented can be found in that book."

Emily shrugged. "Then what are we

waiting for? Let's go look at the book. There must be one that can help you."

"I don't think so," Arden murmured.

"There's no harm in looking." Emily took two steps toward the Emerald Palace. "Come on!"

Arden shook her long white mane. "It's too dangerous. My horn lost its magic because I didn't respect its power. We could make things a lot worse."

"Oh, now you sound like Roxanne," Emily teased. "Look, we'll use the magic just this once. I promise."

Arden backed away from Emily. "I've let you down. Magic can't help me now."

"But that's not true!" Emily cried.

Before the princess could say another word, Arden turned and galloped into the woods.

"Arden, wait!" Emily cried.

Emily listened as the sound of the Unicorn's hooves faded away in the distance.

"Come back!" she shouted. "Please, come back!"

But her calls were answered by silence.

Follow That Unicorn!

 Princess Emily's library lay in the topmost turret of the Emerald Palace. It was one of her favorite places to visit. The library was a great round room with many windows. At each window was a seat for reading. Shelves of books lined the walls.

The Great Book of Magic was a dusty, leather-bound book that sat on a wooden stand at the center of the room. Emily had never really opened it before. As she climbed the circular staircase to the library she wondered why. She'd looked at most of the other books in her library.

Maybe I never really needed to look at The Great Book of Magic *until now*, she thought as she reached for the doorknob.

The instant Emily stepped into the library, she could feel that something was different. *The Great Book of Magic* sat where it always had, but it was no longer covered with dust. A beam of light shone onto its cover. The leather gleamed as if it were brand-new.

Emily felt herself being drawn toward it like a magnet. When she neared *The Great Book of Magic,* she reached her hand toward the cover. It opened on its own!

"What?" Emily gasped, jumping backward.

She watched in amazement as the pages flipped themselves. Suddenly they stopped. Now the light shone on the open page. It was beautifully decorated in swirls of blue, red, and gold.

Emily took a tiny step forward. She read the words at the top of the page out loud. "'Once in a Blue Moon.'"

Emily frowned. What could that mean?

Under the title was a rhyme that looked like a recipe — a recipe for magic.

Friends must come first.
Small must become great.
Mountains must move.
Clouds must part.
Then all will be well in the place of
the heart.

Written in tiny letters beneath the spell was this warning:

For this magic to be true,
You must be in your place of the heart
The first minute of a moon that's blue.

Emily stared at the words until she had memorized them. And then, just as magically as it had opened, the book closed, and the light disappeared.

Emily ran to tell her sisters what had happened. They were still working on the quilt.

The Emerald Princess described the big leather book and recited the words she'd read.

"It definitely sounds like a magic spell," Demetra said. "But what does it mean? Mountains don't move."

"And how can the moon turn blue?" Roxanne asked.

Sabrina finished threading her needle and said, "When I first came to Blue Lake, the Water Sprites told me of it. How every now and then the moon catches the color of the lake and reflects its beautiful blue across the Jewel Kingdom."

"How often does that happen?" Demetra asked, pulling her needle through her patch.

"It's very rare," Sabrina explained. "Only when the full moon falls on the night spring turns to summer."

Emily's big green eyes grew even bigger. "But — but that's — "

She shivered with excitement.

"Tonight!" Demetra and Sabrina cried.

"I have to tell Arden," Emily whispered. "Right away."

"But what makes you think this magic spell will help a Unicorn?" Demetra asked.

"Something happened to Arden, and suddenly *The Great Book of Magic* showed me a spell," Emily explained. "Don't you see? It has to be a magic spell for Unicorns."

"But what if you're wrong?" Sabrina asked.

"I can't be wrong." Emily looked at her sisters. "This is all my fault. Arden wouldn't have lost her magical powers if I hadn't made her use them as a plaything." She clenched her jaw. "I made this mess. I'm going to fix it."

The princess hurried to the sunroom window and whistled. Moments later a furry creature with long arms and a friendly round face swung into the room. It was a Shinnybin.

"At your service, Princess," the Shinnybin said with a grin. "What can I do for you? Take a message to the Jewel Palace? Some herbs to Nana Woodbine? A letter to a friend?"

"I don't need anything delivered, but I do need your help," Emily said. She took a deep breath. "You see, Arden and I were talking a short time ago, and she got very upset about something and galloped away. Could you help me find her?"

The Shinnybin waved one furry arm. "Well, I just saw Arden leaving the Greenwood."

"Where was she going?" Emily asked.

The Shinnybin made a face. "You're not going to like this answer."

"Go ahead and tell me," Emily urged.

"Arden followed the Rushing River straight into the Mysterious Forest," the Shinnybin replied.

"What?!" Emily gasped. "Are you sure about this?"

The Shinnybin put one hand over his heart. "Trust me, Princess. I speak true."

This was terrible news. The Mysterious Forest was a dark line of trees that cut across the heart of the Jewel Kingdom. Emily tried never to go into those woods. Bad things happened there.

"I have to go after her," Emily said in a shaky voice.

"You can't go into that forest," Roxanne said. "Darklings might be there."

The Darklings worked for the evil Lord Bleak. He was the only enemy of the Jewel Kingdom.

"You wouldn't want to run into one of those horrible creatures," Demetra said with a shudder.

"But I have to go," Emily said firmly. "Arden is there."

"Emily is right." Sabrina put down her needle and stood up. "She must go help her friend. A Unicorn without her powers is not safe in that place."

Emily hurried to her room for a knapsack. She packed water, some food, and a few bandages, just in case. She also made sure she was carrying her magic flute. It had the power to make her grow very large or very small.

Emily raced back to say good-bye to her sisters. Demetra caught hold of her arm. "Emily, wait! We should go with you!"

Emily shook her head. "Thank you,

but I know I must help Arden all by myself."

"But how are you going to help Arden?" Demetra asked as Emily ran out the palace door.

"With the magic spell," Emily shouted over her shoulder.

Demetra ran to the door and called, "But you don't even know what it means!"

Emily shrugged. "I'll figure it out."

Then the Emerald Princess raced to the Mysterious Forest.

Trapped!

 With her shoulders back and her head held high, Princess Emily marched straight into the Mysterious Forest. She was trying her hardest to look brave.

Emily followed a winding path that led over rotted stumps and under twisted, hanging vines. Each step took her farther and farther away from the golden light of the Greenwood and into the dark gloom of the Mysterious Forest.

Every few feet Emily would stop and call, "Arden? Are you here?"

Once she was answered by the loud squawk of a dark-winged bird. Another time several twigs cracked and she was sure she heard footsteps running into the dense thicket.

Suddenly, Emily spied a strange little wagon blocking the path ahead of her. It was piled high with rags, rusty tools, and tattered leather books.

The owner of the wagon didn't appear to be nearby. Just to be safe, Emily left the path and tiptoed through the brush.

As she got closer to the wagon, Emily heard squeaky voices. They were snorting with laughter at something.

The princess crept to the edge of a

clearing behind the wagon. She saw small furry creatures in leather pants and vests. They were only half Emily's height and had long, spiky teeth and sharp claws. All of them wore masks to cover their eyes and carried slingshots in their paws.

"Jibbets!" Emily murmured. She'd never actually met a Jibbet, but she'd seen drawings of them. They were greedy little creatures who roamed the world stealing anything they could lay their claws on.

The Jibbets had formed a tight circle around something on the far side of the clearing. The light was very dim. Emily peered through the bushes to see what they had found.

She glimpsed a flash of white mane over the Jibbets' heads.

"Oh, no!" Emily gasped. The creatures had cornered Arden!

The Emerald Princess dropped her pack and scurried along the side of the clearing. When she was only a few feet from the Jibbets, she heard a voice order, "Give us the horn or we'll take it!"

Arden's beautiful brown eyes were filled with fear. "Please," she said softly. "My horn has lost its magic. It is of no use to you."

"That's a lie!" another Jibbet shrieked. "A Unicorn's horn is the best magic there is. I say we break off the horn and be done with it!"

Emily's face clouded with anger. Those terrible little Jibbets were going to take Arden's beautiful horn. And the Unicorn was helpless to stop them.

Emily could stand it no longer. She sprang from the bushes and landed directly in front of the Jibbets.

"If any of you even touches this Unicorn," she said in her loudest voice, "you'll have to answer to me!"

"You?" a short, round Jibbet sneered. "Who are you?"

Emily put her hands on her hips and tilted her chin high. "I am the Emerald Princess, daughter of King Regal and Queen Jemma, and ruler of the Greenwood."

"The Emerald Princess!" the Jibbet repeated in surprise.

He quickly turned back to talk to the other Jibbets.

Arden touched Emily with her nose. "Princess, you shouldn't be here."

"I found *The Great Book of Magic*," Emily whispered over her shoulder. "There's a spell in there that I know will help you. But we have to go to your place of the heart by tonight. Do you know where that might be?"

Arden didn't hesitate. "The Land of the Unicorns."

Before Arden could explain, the leader of the Jibbets spun to face the princess. "Well, Princess Emily of the Greenwood, do you have any idea where you are?"

Emily tossed her red hair over her shoulder. "Of course I do. We're in the Mysterious Forest."

"That's right." He smiled, baring his yellow, spiky teeth. "You have no power here."

"Listen, you." She bent down low so that her face was right in front of his. "You are making me very angry," she hissed. "And when I get angry — look out!"

The Jibbet stared up at Emily. Then his eyes grew very wide. He squealed in fright and so did the rest of the Jibbets. Suddenly Jibbets were running everywhere. They grabbed Emily's knapsack and their wagon, and vanished into the forest.

"That's telling them," Arden said in amazement.

Emily cocked her head. She knew she had sounded fierce. But not *that* fierce. What made the Jibbets run away?

The princess turned to look at the Unicorn and her question was answered. There, pressed between two very tall trees, was a huge, scowling face.

"Arden, look out!" Emily yelled. "It's a Giant!"

A Big Surprise!

 The Giant reached one huge hand out of the treetops and grabbed Arden. He lifted her high above Princess Emily's head.

"Oh, dear," Arden gasped. "What shall I do?"

"Don't worry, Arden," Emily cried. "I'll save you!"

The princess reached for her magic

flute. It hung on a cord over her shoulder. The great wizard Gallivant had given it to Emily the day she was crowned the Emerald Princess. If she blew the highest note, she became very small. If she blew the lowest note on her flute, she would grow very big.

Emily took a deep breath and blew the low note.

In an instant she became as tall as an evergreen tree.

She found herself staring into a pair of very blue eyes. The Giant blinked at Emily, then showed her the Unicorn. "See? Horsie!"

"Horsie?" Emily repeated, staring down at Arden.

The Giant grinned. He had one tooth at the top of his mouth and one on the bottom. "Scrub likes horsies!"

Emily was amazed. This wasn't a big scary Giant. This was a baby.

"Well, hello there, Scrub," the princess said, smiling back at the baby Giant. "I'm Emily. Could I see your horsie?"

Scrub nodded and handed Emily the Unicorn. Arden had been very still so the Giant wouldn't drop her.

"Don't be afraid," Emily said to Arden as she held her in her hands. "I've got you now."

"Thank you, Princess," Arden called with relief.

Then the princess walked to the edge of the Mysterious Forest and knelt on the grass. She very carefully set Arden on the ground.

Scrub toddled after Emily and knelt beside her. "Do you like my horsie?" he asked.

Emily smiled at Scrub. "Very much," she said. "But this isn't a toy horse, Scrub. This is a magical Unicorn. You have to be very careful not to touch her. You might hurt her."

Scrub puffed out his lower lip in a pout. "I want my horsie." Then he added, "I want my mommy!"

Emily hadn't seen any sign of Scrub's parents. She stood up and looked back into the forest. Then she looked the other way, across the meadow.

"I don't see your mommy, Scrub," she said. "Do you know where she might be?"

"Home!" Scrub's chin began to quiver. "I want to go home."

Emily leaned down to speak to Arden. "Where do you think Scrub's parents might be?"

"Crumble Canyon," the Unicorn replied. "Most Giants live there."

Emily tilted up her head at the baby Giant. "Scrub? Do you live in Crumble Canyon?"

"Yes!" Scrub grinned and hopped up and down so hard the ground shook.

"We had better take him home," Arden called, "before his parents notice he's missing and get upset."

Emily frowned. "But we can't take him home. If we go to Crumble Canyon, we won't make it to the Land of the Unicorns before moonrise."

"I don't understand," Arden said. "Why do we need to be there so soon?"

Emily realized she hadn't told Arden everything about the magic spell. "The words in the book were very clear." She recited them from memory: "'For this magic to be true, you must be in your place of the heart the first minute of a moon that's blue.'" Then Emily added, "And that's tonight."

"Then what happens?" Arden asked.

Emily sighed impatiently. "We have to do a few tasks. And then you'll get your magic powers back."

Arden looked doubtful. "My place of the heart is the Land of the Unicorns. But I don't know if we can even get to it."

"Why?"

"Because it's a very special place, high in the mountains, wrapped in the clouds. Only the oldest and wisest Unicorns have earned the right to live there. The rest of us can visit from time to time, but only on special occasions."

"I can't think of a more special occasion than this," Emily said firmly. "Come on."

The Unicorn looked up at Scrub. Two big tears were rolling down his cheeks. "Princess," Arden said, "I think we need to take Scrub back to his parents."

"But what about your magic powers?" Emily asked.

"I can live without my powers," Arden replied. "But can you?"

Emily knelt beside the Unicorn. "Of course I can," she whispered. "Your magic isn't what makes you special. You are special on your own!"

Arden lowered her head. "But my magic seems so important to you. You like to use my magic to light your way through the forest. You like to see me fly. How will you feel when I can't do those things?"

"I'll feel fine," Emily declared. "Oh, Arden, I only wanted the magic back because I thought you did! I know this is all my fault. You lost your magic because I made you do silly tricks for me with it. But I don't care about the magic. I just want my dearest friend to be happy again."

"Are you certain of this?" Arden asked.

Emily placed one hand over her heart. "I swear."

Arden tossed her long mane of hair. "Then what are we waiting for? Let's take this baby home."

Emily grinned. "All right, friend. If that's what you want."

"It is," Arden said firmly.

"Mommy," Scrub whimpered. "Where is my mommy?"

Emily leaped to her feet and took Scrub by the hand.

"We're going to take you to your mommy this minute. And if you're very good, I'll bet Arden will let you carry her to your house."

Scrub's tears dried instantly. "I'll be good. Please, let me carry the horsie."

Emily carefully placed Arden in Scrub's open palm and they started on their way to Crumble Canyon.

As the three of them crossed Buttercup Meadow, Arden looked up at Emily and whispered, "I just have one little question."

"What's that?" Emily asked.

"If Scrub is a baby Giant, how big are his parents?"

Emily looked at Scrub and gulped. "Too big."

Meet the Giants

 The path Princess Emily and Scrub were following turned into a very wide road. Scrub recognized it and gurgled with joy. "Home. We're home!"

Scrub skipped down the road as fast as he could. Emily raced to keep up with him. She was afraid he was going to drop Arden. She had to take care of her friend.

"I'll hold the horsie while you run," Emily said.

Once Scrub handed Arden to the princess, he bolted for several huge rocks that lined the side of the road.

Emily followed him. But when she rounded the bend, there was no one in sight.

"If this is a land of Giants," she murmured to Arden, "where are all of the people? This place looks deserted."

Suddenly, the mountains on either side of the road began to shake and come to life.

"Are you the thief who stole my baby?" a voice roared from high above Emily.

Emily tilted back her head and gasped. The two big rocks weren't mountains, they were Scrub's mother and father. The mother was holding Scrub in her arms. She scowled down at Emily with huge, stony gray eyes. "Now you'll find out what Giants do to baby-stealers."

"I didn't steal Scrub," Emily shouted up to the Giants. "I found him in the Mysterious Forest. Or rather, he found me. You see, I am the Emerald Princess, ruler of the Greenwood."

Scrub's mother squinted her eyes at Emily and then turned to her husband, who stood beside her. "She says she's the Emerald Princess. What do you think, Mr. Rumple?"

The Giant stared at Emily. "She's dressed like a princess. She acts like a princess." Then he shook his head. "But she's too big, Mrs. Rumple."

Emily looked down at herself. She'd forgotten that she was bigger than her normal size. "You're right, I am big," she sputtered. "But that's because I used my magic flute. I blew the low note and grew large."

"Then blow another note and grow small," Mr. Rumple ordered.

Emily pursed her lips. "I can't," she said. "It doesn't work that way."

Whenever she used her magic flute, Emily had to stay at whatever size she had become until sundown. That meant she was going to be a Giant for a little while longer.

Mr. Rumple frowned, squeezing his big, bushy eyebrows together. "I think you're lying."

"But I'm not," Emily protested. "Ask Scrub how we met."

The Giant turned to look at Scrub, but he had fallen fast asleep against Mrs. Rumple's shoulder.

Emily was still holding Arden in her hands. She bent her head low to whisper to the Unicorn. "What can I say to convince him?"

"I'm not sure," Arden replied. "Can you wait until sundown when you change back to your normal size?"

Emily looked up at the sky. The sun was about to set but it would be a few more minutes before it disappeared.

"I don't know," she whispered. "Mr. Rumple seems awfully upset."

"Who are you talking to?" the Giant asked.

Emily shielded Arden with her arm. "My friend Arden the Unicorn. She lives with me at the Emerald Palace."

"A Unicorn?" Mr. Rumple held out his hand. "Let me see it."

The princess didn't want to hand

Arden to the Giant. What if he hurt her?

"Go ahead, Princess," Arden called. "He might believe you if he sees me."

Emily very carefully placed the Unicorn onto the Giant's palm.

Mr. Rumple raised his hand so that Arden was eye level with him. "Well, I'll be," he murmured. "You *are* a Unicorn."

Arden extended her front leg and bowed her head. "Pleased to meet you, Mr. Rumple. I am Arden the Unicorn. I serve Princess Emily of the Greenwood."

Scrub's mother nudged her husband. "A Unicorn would never lie. Perhaps that girl *is* the princess, Mr. Rumple."

"I promise you I am," Emily said, watching the sun as it headed for the horizon. "And if you'll just wait a few minutes, I'll prove it."

"What are you doing so far from the

Greenwood?" Mr. Rumple asked as he put Arden down gently.

Emily quickly explained that Arden's horn had lost its magical power. She told Mr. and Mrs. Rumple about *The Great Book of Magic* and the spell she had found. Then she told them about the Jibbets and discovering Scrub in the Mysterious Forest.

"We were just about to go to the Land of the Unicorns when Scrub started crying," Emily said. "Arden and I decided it was best to bring him home."

"But what about the magic spell and the Land of the Unicorns?" Mrs. Rumple asked.

"Oh, that." Emily waved one hand. "It's too late for that."

"Maybe not," Mr. Rumple said. "Tell us about this spell."

Emily quickly recited it for them. "*'Friends must come first. Small must become great. Mountains must move. Clouds must part. Then all will be well in the place of the heart.'*"

"Hmmm." Mr. Rumple tapped his chin. "That's an interesting spell."

"It's very complicated," Emily said. "None of those things has happened and our time is almost up."

"Wait a minute," Arden said suddenly. "You put friends first when you came to help me."

"And so did you, Arden," Emily replied. "When you chose to help Scrub instead of yourself."

The Giant raised an eyebrow. "What about the rest of the spell?"

"'Small must become great,'" Emily murmured. "What could that mean?"

Arden cocked her head. "Well, you did blow your flute and go from being very small to very large."

Mrs. Rumple nodded. "That fits."

Arden paced in a small circle. "What about mountains moving? We definitely didn't see that."

Emily's eyes widened. "I did!" she cried. "When we first entered Crumble Canyon, I thought Scrub's parents were mountains. Then they moved!"

"Very good!" Arden cried. "Oh, Princess, we've completed all of our tasks. Maybe the spell will work after all."

"If we get to the Land of the Unicorns in time," Emily reminded her.

"Should we try?" Arden asked.

"Of course!" Emily said. "We've come so far, Arden, we can't stop now. Not when we're so close."

Arden smiled. "All right. But if I do get my magic back, I promise never to use it to show off again."

"Me, too," Emily agreed with a big smile.

Emily was grinning at Arden when the sun disappeared behind the hills. Suddenly Emily shrank back to her normal size.

"Oh, no! We're too late," she cried from the ground far below the Giants. "The sun has set and we haven't finished the spell."

"What is left to do?" Mr. Rumple asked.

"The clouds must part and we must speak this spell in the Land of the Unicorns. But it's so far from here."

"Not to a Giant," Mr. Rumple said with a grin. "I can take you there in a minute. In less than a minute."

The Emerald Princess looked up at the sky. She didn't know if they'd make it before moonrise. But it was worth a try. "Let's go!" she cried.

Before Emily could say "blue moon," Mr. Rumple had scooped her into the palm of his hand. She clung to Arden's neck as he lifted them higher and higher into the clouds.

The Great Unicorn

 Mr. Rumple set Princess Emily and the Unicorn down on a thin rock ledge. Thick clouds swirled around it. Then he said farewell and disappeared.

Emily looked at the misty world around her. She couldn't tell if they were on land or high up in the sky. "Arden, where are we?"

"This is my place of the heart,"

Arden answered softly. "The Land of the Unicorns."

Suddenly a beautiful halo of light broke through the mist and the clouds parted.

A great white Unicorn galloped toward Emily and Arden. When he was just in front of them, he reared up on his hind legs and whinnied loudly.

Emily had never seen a creature so magnificent in her entire life. She huddled next to Arden, not knowing whether to be happy or scared.

"Wh-who is that?" she whispered.

"The Great Unicorn," Arden replied as she bowed her head. "The ruler of all Unicorns."

Princess Emily curtsied low.

The Great Unicorn greeted them and then stood on a platform of white marble.

He spoke in a stern voice. "You two are here for a reason. Do you know what it is?"

"Yes, sir," Emily said shakily. "We're here because Arden has lost her magic powers."

The Great Unicorn lowered his head to look at Emily. "Do you know why her powers are gone?"

The Emerald Princess stared at the ground. "I think they disappeared because of me," she confessed. "I asked Arden to perform magic tricks just for the fun of it. Not because we needed the magic."

The Great Unicorn nodded. "Magic is a precious gift. There is only so much of it in this world. We must be very careful not to waste it."

Emily forced herself to look the Great Unicorn in the eye. "I was the one who wasted the magic," she said boldly. "And

I'm the one who should pay for it. Not Arden."

The Great Unicorn looked at Arden. "Do you agree with this princess?"

Arden shook her head. "Not completely. We're both at fault. The princess asked me to perform magic tricks, but I did them because I liked showing off. I didn't treasure the gift I had been given."

Emily wrapped her arm around Arden's neck and begged, "Please, sir. We've learned our lesson. Is there any way that Arden can get her powers back?"

The Great Unicorn tilted his head. "Why, does she need them?"

"Well, . . ." Emily stopped and thought for a moment. Then she said simply, "She doesn't *need* them. We'll be perfectly happy together without being able to fly. Or walk home at night by the light of her horn. But they're part of who Arden is. A Unicorn. Having them back would make her feel good about herself again."

Arden nudged Emily with her nose. "I'm happy now."

Emily smiled. "Then I'm happy, too."

The Great Unicorn looked at the sky. The outline of the full moon shone brightly above them. "The blue moon is just beginning," he said.

Emily faced Arden. "We're not too late. Quick!" she whispered. "Let's repeat the spell."

The Unicorn and the Emerald Princess recited the words from *The Great Book of Magic*:

"Friends must come first.
Small must become great.
Mountains must move.

Clouds must part.
Then all will be well in the place of
the heart."

But nothing happened.

"Do you feel any different?" Emily asked Arden.

Arden shook her head. "No, Princess," she said softly. "I feel just the same."

Princess Emily looked up at the Great Unicorn, who had been watching them in silence. He seemed so big and strong. Why couldn't he give back Arden's magic? *Maybe*, she thought sadly, *he doesn't have the power to undo what we have done.*

Emily buried her face in Arden's mane. "Arden, we did our best, and that is what matters. We're still the best of friends."

"And will always be," Arden replied.

Emily grinned. "Who needs all that silly old magic anyway?"

Arden tossed her head. "Not me!"

"Tomorrow is the quilt presentation at the Jewel Palace," Emily reminded Arden. "I haven't even started my patch."

"Then we had better hurry home!" Arden said.

The princess and Arden bowed to the Great Unicorn and set off down the mountain for home. They were disappointed, but anxious to return to the Greenwood.

The Magic Returns

The next day, Princess Emily and Arden rode to the Jewel Palace. Emily had stayed up all night sewing her patch. When she arrived at the Jewel Palace, she hurried to the room where the quilt was being kept and quickly attached her square.

Princess Demetra begged to have a look at it. "Just one peek?" she asked.

Emily was firm. "It's a secret. You'll see it at the presentation."

Queen Jemma and King Regal entered their throne room and a trumpet sounded on the far side of the palace.

"That's for us," Princess Sabrina told her sisters. "It's time to present our quilt."

The four sisters marched into the throne room and carefully unrolled their gift. The quilt was beautiful. Princess Roxanne spoke to their parents first.

"This quilt honors your anniversary and tells the story of your four daughters. We have each made a patch showing something special about our lands. We give it to you with love."

Roxanne showed her patch. She had sewn the Ruby Palace perched high in the Red Mountains. Hapgood the Dragon stood on the steps of the palace with his wings spread wide.

Princess Sabrina was next. Her patch showed Water Sprites diving over a rainbow in Blue Lake. Behind them was Bluebonnet Falls. "My world of water and sunshine is filled with rainbows," she explained.

Demetra's patch captured a moment of the Winter Fair in the White Winterland. "This is my favorite celebration in my land," she told her parents. "I look forward to it all year."

Now it was Emily's turn. Her patchwork piece was a little loose and she quickly sewed down the corner with one last stitch. "Sorry," she said, her face turning red. "I just finished it."

King Regal and Queen Jemma smiled

at their daughter. "Tell us about your patch," the king urged.

Emily stepped back so that her sisters and all of the guests could see what she had sewn. There was no palace or picture of the Greenwood. Not even a special event from her land.

Emily's patch was very simple. It was a picture of Emily with her arm draped over Arden the Unicorn's neck.

"Arden is the most important part of my kingdom," she explained. "We're not doing anything magical on my patch, just being best friends."

Then Emily crossed to Arden, who was standing in the crowd. "You see, I've learned that the best magic of all is the magic of friendship." She beamed at the Unicorn. "And that's all this princess will ever need."

Arden playfully nudged Emily with her horn. Suddenly the horn began to glow.

"Would you look at that!" Princess Sabrina cried.

Emily turned and gasped, "Arden! Your magic is back!"

The horn's brilliant light filled the throne room. Everyone was grinning. But no one was happier than the Emerald Princess.

She flung her arms around Arden's neck and cried, "It worked! The spell really worked!"

Arden whispered, "And that's the last time we'll use a magic spell to solve our problems. Right, Princess?"

Emily winked at the Unicorn. "Right, Arden."

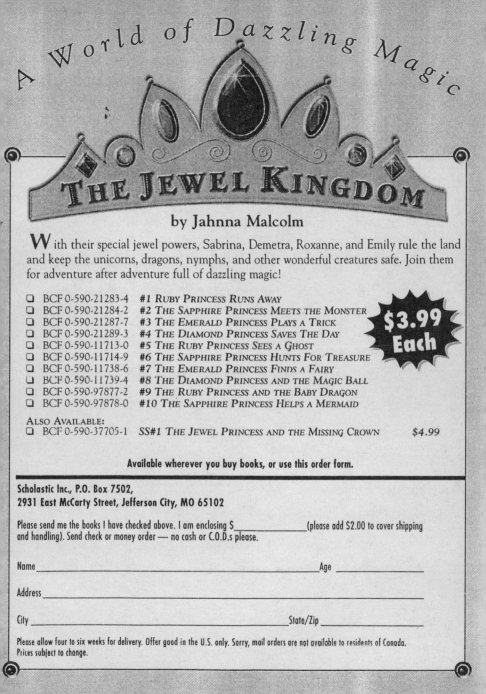

A World of Dazzling Magic

THE JEWEL KINGDOM

by Jahnna Malcolm

With their special jewel powers, Sabrina, Demetra, Roxanne, and Emily rule the land and keep the unicorns, dragons, nymphs, and other wonderful creatures safe. Join them for adventure after adventure full of dazzling magic!

- ❑ BCF 0-590-21283-4   **#1 RUBY PRINCESS RUNS AWAY**
- ❑ BCF 0-590-21284-2   **#2 THE SAPPHIRE PRINCESS MEETS THE MONSTER**
- ❑ BCF 0-590-21287-7   **#3 THE EMERALD PRINCESS PLAYS A TRICK**
- ❑ BCF 0-590-21289-3   **#4 THE DIAMOND PRINCESS SAVES THE DAY**
- ❑ BCF 0-590-11713-0   **#5 THE RUBY PRINCESS SEES A GHOST**
- ❑ BCF 0-590-11714-9   **#6 THE SAPPHIRE PRINCESS HUNTS FOR TREASURE**
- ❑ BCF 0-590-11738-6   **#7 THE EMERALD PRINCESS FINDS A FAIRY**
- ❑ BCF 0-590-11739-4   **#8 THE DIAMOND PRINCESS AND THE MAGIC BALL**
- ❑ BCF 0-590-97877-2   **#9 THE RUBY PRINCESS AND THE BABY DRAGON**
- ❑ BCF 0-590-97878-0   **#10 THE SAPPHIRE PRINCESS HELPS A MERMAID**

$3.99 Each

ALSO AVAILABLE:
- ❑ BCF 0-590-37705-1   *SS#1 THE JEWEL PRINCESS AND THE MISSING CROWN* $4.99

Available wherever you buy books, or use this order form.

Scholastic Inc., P.O. Box 7502,
2931 East McCarty Street, Jefferson City, MO 65102

Please send me the books I have checked above. I am enclosing $_____(please add $2.00 to cover shipping and handling). Send check or money order — no cash or C.O.D.s please.

Name _____ Age _____

Address _____

City _____ State/Zip _____

Please allow four to six weeks for delivery. Offer good in the U.S. only. Sorry, mail orders are not available to residents of Canada. Prices subject to change.

JK898